DAMNED COWS!

JOTTINGS AND CONFESSIONS OF A FARMER'S WIFE

JILL DUDLEY

Published by
Orpington Publishers
Email: info@orpingtonpublishers.co.uk

Originated and printed by
Creeds Design and Print,
Bridport, Dorset
01308 423411

ISBN 9781-0686883-1-7

CONTENTS

PROLOGUE

I swore I would never marry a farmer, and I never did. I married an oil executive – a fine title for a young man working for an oil company. We had a large wedding with all the trimmings as befitted the daughter of a London bank manager marrying an oil executive whose parents had a manor house in Suffolk.

And we lived happily ever after…

Five years on and two infants down the line the young executive was made redundant as his company was closing down its overseas offices.

"I've always wanted to farm," he said. That was news to me as he had never said a word about it in the past. But he had always given me encouragement in my aspirations to be a writer as well as learning Greek, and I felt I should be as supportive of him in his desire to be a farmer.

"So long as I'm not your farm labourer," I said.

"No, of course not! You, my labourer? I wouldn't dream of it!"

And so he did an agricultural course.

People said it would be foolhardy to buy a farm without at least thirty thousand pounds behind us. We had seven thousand only. We bought a farm of one hundred acres for twelve thousand pounds. The year was 1964.

The bank dealt kindly with us and we had good health.– the greatest requirements for any farming family. My oil executive husband, now a farmer, was damned if he would be beaten by cows, by muck, or by a wife who did not want to be his labourer; the whole enterprise was a huge challenge in endurance, resourcefulness and patience.

What follows are the jottings of a farmer's wife who never wanted to be one, but who did her best under adverse, trying and often very demanding circumstances.

SONG OF THE FARMER'S WIFE

Oh, in this scientific age, this age of energy, is there no other way of getting milk for human needs than from a cow? The cow who contemplates indifferently her slave who labours every day to keep her?

Oh, is there no engine? No engine, lightly oiled or functioning by winds or tides, able to pour milk into a bottle? A machine of cogs and wheels which can whirr daily into action, without heart or guts or stomach? Which cannot dung or piss, does not need the service of a bull, will not conceive to drop a calf inconveniently in some far field – will not kick – will not die –

The ancient Greeks sacrificed their cattle to their gods. Now the cattle, with supercilious airs, watch the farmer sacrifice himself!

This modern tale is of a man who, born a gentleman, chose to put away the things of gentlemen to become a farmer. His city suits were hung in cupboards for the moth, and on his legs he wore blue-jeans, and on his chest a tattered shirt. His hands, once slender, manicured and elegant, grew calloused, coarse and swollen.

'Book-farmer' he was known as locally. The neighbours gossiped and placed bets, giving him three years before the farm would break him. They watched him flex his muscles, set his jaw and buy a tractor and some cows. They watched and waited, gleefully flexing their own hairy arms, stroking their hoary faces, waiting – watching –

Farming is a way of life – or death.

The farmer had a wife. Born and bred a Londoner, the woman knew the pleasures of a flippant life. Alas, she was not born of farming stock. Reading books, learning Greek and strumming the guitar were her recreations.

Beware all farmers who would choose a bride! Go to the market and select a girl who is a farmer's daughter. Look her over well and judge her as you would a tractor. A farmer's wife should have a skin of lead, and bones of steel in order to withstand hard blows from metal pipes and concrete blocks...She should not be soft-spoken but possess tough lungs like leather bellows, giving her the power to shout messages, horning them like a bugle across fields, and enabling her too to run long distances. The ideal farmer's wife is placid so that nothing ruffles her. A farmer's wife should not be feminine at all, yet woman enough to bear sons:small babies with monstrous potential – the labourers of tomorrow.

Who would be a farmer's wife?

Who would be a farmer's son?

Who would be a farmer?

The farmer thought that everything he did was due to his own brawn and brain. He did not know a Goddess, living high above the hill, bestowed on him her patronage. Many were the times the Goddess helped the farmer. She stayed his hand when bidding at an auction for some cow with large, full udder but with old and overgrown hoof concealed in straw. She rescued him from overturning on his tractor, supporting him with mighty strength until the wheels that were uplifted in the air returned to solid ground. She brought the vet, driving him magically at high speeds to the farm to save a cow as good as dead. She did a multitude of things and under her care and guidance the farm flourished. Commonly to all around she was known as the Goddess Muck. Under her patronage milk flowed.

The cows with placid unconcern allowed this farmer to fulfil his obligations to them daily. Willingly he worked for them. Ruminating with self-satisfaction the cows made great demands upon their slave and threatened to withhold their milk if anything upset them. He, knowing their displeasure meant his loss, toiled the more to please each one. Mark well who was the boss! Oh, workers, listen! Take heed! No member of a union has such power! Oh, clever cow! Behind that countenance of large-eyed somnolence a tyrant! And yet this farmer thought that he was free! He happily believed it:free enterprise! Oh, wicked words!

Typical was the evening when the cattle cried to heaven, lowing in confused supplication because they found themselves upon the road, distressed and running haphazardly before a car. The farmer's wife learned of it by telephone from a sorrowfully chuckling neighbour.

The Goddess Muck, asleep upon the hillside, was woken suddenly by these bellowing cattle and the chortling dialect of the locals shortening the odds as they drank their ale. They had laid bets the farmer's wife would soon be gone. Knowing their thoughts the Goddess Muck quickly set herself to help the woman. Swiftly descending to her side she disguised her as a raging wind and sent her whirling over hill and dale, up over hedges, leaping across ditches, breasting the steepest slopes until, on finding the lowing cattle, she reassumed the mortal figure of the angry farmer's wife:red faced, gum-booted, swearing, sweating and waving a stick.

Time passed, year upon year. Smiling, our farmer bounced about the fields upon his tractor. Smiling, he milked his cows, and their daughters and their grand-daughters. His neighbours settled their bets and grudgingly admired the farmer's skill at overcoming crises.

Not knowing that the Goddess Muck had helped him, the farmer thought himself the reigning champion of the countryside. He was supreme! All was under his control he thought:the farm, the cattle and his wife! Oh, monstrous pride! He had not thanked the Goddess once – he had not got the time or eyes to see that she was even there to thank!

The Goddess grew annoyed with his ingratitude. One day she sat alone upon her cloud, her eyes glazed, her bottom lip petulant. She stared idly at the world and her glance chanced upon the farmer smiling to himself. His happiness irritated her. Raising an arm, the Goddess tossed a storm and waited…When the winds and clouds dispersed she saw the farmer busily at work, replacing slates, repairing fences, rodding drains – in short, he went on farming.

Angered by his obstinate ability the Goddess Muck mused inwardly and then conceived a long-term plan which promised her much entertainment. She caused the farmer's wife to languish, and yearn for something more – anything – anything to bring her change from buckets, brooms and bales of hay.

The Goddess searched the area with perceptive wickedness until upon a nearby hill she saw a housetop sheltered by some trees, surrounding which were rhododendron bushes with large blooms both red and pink. There another married couple lived and the wife, fancying herself upon a horse, rode often. When dismounted she walked dogs and hatched ducks and geese. There the husband stood long-limbed, playing a guitar; and sometimes he sat and strummed the piano. The Goddess Muck's brow cleared wonderfully.

She sat the woman on her horse and fixed a mirage to her eyes and sent her trotting distantly searching for she knew not what. At the same instant the young musician, wanting some employment, placed an advert in the local paper announcing himself a teacher of the guitar. Then, flying to the farmer's wife, the Goddess dropped a philtre in her drink which caused her to want lessons so she could improve on the instrument. The rhododendrons bloomed marvellously, throwing round the tutor's house their unaffected charm.

And so the tutor and the farmer's wife did meet. He instructed her upon the guitar until each solemn note she plucked sounded divine. Sometimes he played to her and she was amazed at the dexterity with which he fingered. the strings producing resonant notes. Often they played together, he believing that he taught and she that she was learning from him.

With fiendish zeal the Goddess Muck pursued her plans. One day she saw the tutor's wife go hacking off upon her cob, following her mirage. The Goddess Muck swept down and touched the cob upon its rump with firebrands. With a wild lurch the beast leapt forward at the gallop, unseating his mount who, clutching neck and mane slipped sideways from the saddle, lost stirrup, reins and balance, and soon obeyed the laws of gravity, alas.

Her wicked deed accomplished, the Goddess Muck found her quick way back, past large flowered rhododendron bushes, to the house where the farmer's wife and tutor played duets together. There she spun a web of charm and magic round the two musicians. Spinning and spinning, the Goddess wove her web tighter round the tutor and the farmer's wife. Tighter and tighter spun the web until, lo! the tutor with his mind afire quite lost his head. The farmer's wife, also with new alighted senses, swooned and, suddenly, they erred quite shockingly together. All was over before hardly it had started. So swiftly was it done that, to be certain it had ever happened, they promised themselves more sweet orchestral sessions.

Some time later the cob returned with broken rein and saddle all askew. Hanging his head he champed away along the grass verge of the driveway. Later still, the tutor's wife limped home, tired and irritable. Irritated she was with husband, horse and home. Oh, untamed shrew! When charms have been enjoyed what husband wants to stay to suffer aggravations from a wife?

The Goddess Muck was much amused by this human entertainment. She laughed aloud at all the folly. Her merriment came like strong gusts of wind which rocked the rooks high in the trees and set them calling raucously.

The Goddess Muck now taught the farmer's wife artifice and cunning. She taught her to listen for the different sounds machinery makes upon a farm, as though they were the songs of birds heard through the changing seasons:she learned the steady beat of baling on a summer's day, the gobbling of a hedge-cutter in autumn and the high flicking sound of muck-spreading in winter.

Hearing these machine-calls the wife would waste long hours upon the telephone, and many more in sighing. At the ceasing of the engines the kindly Goddess then helped her speedily perform the tasks a farmer's wife should do each day. On entering, the farmer found her busy at her wifely chores such as cooking, cleaning the house, the dairy, fetching the cows, feeding the calves, the dogs, the cats and so on.

Still the farm flourished, and still the farmer thought himself supreme. The Goddess had her plans, and now she swept the sky of clouds and caused a drought. She would have the farmer on his knees; she would have him taught that his success was due in greater part to her.

The Goddess Muck was cruel. She filed her nails and sharpened them like talons. She kept the sky swept clear of clouds and polished up the sun until it gleamed more brilliantly each day. The grass withered and grew brown; scorched fields and dry water-beds were now the scene.

Ah, the weather!

The farmer groaned. Oh, hapless man, dependent not upon himself but on the sky! Now that the weather was bad (in agriculture bad means too much sun as well as too much rain) now it was bad he belaboured his wife daily with his plaints. He hooked his ear to the radio where it stayed like a small cap on a peg while he listened to the forecasts. Tormented when they were right, tormented when they were not, he ground his teeth and grumbled with never flagging, burbling, babbling, brow-bashing, drought-drenching, punch-driving, drivelling futility.

The farmer's wife fretted. She longed to hear guitars but instead heard only the farmer's blithering, blathering complaints about the cloudless sky, the sun, the drought – The farmer had much to grumble at but too much faith in the capacity of his wife to listen

Gossip spread. Neighbouring heads bowed to heads, mouths whispered into ears in sitting-rooms and parlours, over hedges, across ditches, between bar-stools and by telephone. The news was that the farmer's wife was often taking lessons on the guitar; that so much time passed at the tutor's house and music was not always heard and the silence, yes, the silence, ah, the silence! What possibilities lie in silence! Gossip, like gnats, filled the warm air, circling and spreading in soft clouds.

One hot and windless day the cows lined up for milking in the yard like workmen on the picket line chewing gum. Food was short; they received too little return for their produce; the unanimous decision was they would withhold their milk.

That evening the farmer lashed his wife with more dry mouthfuls of pent up, stressful, struggling, sermonising, unscintillating, sibilant swipes at the sky, the cows, the withered grass, the parched earth's crust – The Goddess Muck watched the scene with telescopic eye. She watched with bated breath and then with pleasure as the wife's nerves snapped.

Screaming, weeping and gesticulating, the farmer's wife fled suddenly from farmer, cows and forecasts. The Goddess Muck was ready for her flight and lifted her away, sweeping her off as a helicopter might hoist a figure from the edge of an abyss. She carried her across the wooded valleys and set her gently down amongst the rhododendron bushes.

The tutor was surprised to see the farmer's wife. Distraught, she stood before him gabbling incoherent words about caring not for clouds or sunshine, cows or carcasses, hot air or husbands.

His wife had just gone jogging off upon the cob, taking her shrewish temper with her like a knapsack. She let her irritation fly in all directions with her switch. Over all the jumps the poor beast leaped, trying to escape her voice and stinging blows. She stayed aloft, urging him on indomitably, sharpening her will against his unwillingness. How could she get such satisfaction from a husband who responded only with soft music?

Too readily the tutor listened to the sobbing farmer's wife. Too willingly he wiped her tears and laid aside the problems which he knew – to take up others.

Niggling, naggling, the tutor's wife rode home refreshed, to find her husband gone.

The cob trembled.

Now the fiendish neighbours all swooped down like bright-eyed magpies. Drawing near by leaps and bounds they made a banquet of the scandal. Tearing at each titbit they tasted it with relish, consuming it, regurgitating it, consuming it again, until all was finally digested and everyone was fully satisfied.

The Goddess Muck turned back towards the farm. Victoriously she watched the farmer now. With powerless rage the reigning champion of the countryside sobbed as though a multiple of marbles filled his throat. Gulping, he walked amongst his cows. The torrid air fanned his burning face. The brown grass in the fields was as tinder. There the cows all stood watching him, each one mouthing her complaints; mouthing her demands silently. Yes, there they all stood mouthing at him silently.

And suddenly he knew! He was their victim! False wretches! Were they not the cause of all his troubles? Was not the weather his concern because he wished to feed them well? Without them would his wife have fled?

Triumphantly the Goddess Muck looked on and saw the farmer telephone the knacker's yard. By evening every cow was hanging from a hook! That very night the

Goddess Muck sent rain.
Too late! the cows were gone!
Too late! the wife was gone as well!
Oh, God! Oh, Man! Oh, Wife! Oh, Cow!

THE OLYMPIAN VISIT

Because the Goddess Muck watched over the farmer and his wife and knew the woman studied Greek and was interested in the old Olympian gods, one day she daringly took herself off to Mt. Olympus to see them for herself. And there, high on the craggy peaks, she found that band of Greek immortals. The Goddess Muck was humbled by the sight and quaked in her immortal shoes.

Seeing her, the great Lord Zeus laughed aloud and extended his almighty hand in welcome and, together with his ox-eyed, white-armed wife, the beautiful immortal Hera, they offered her their hospitality.

What hospitality! What merry entertainment, and what interest shown in the distant island of Great Britain from which they learned the Goddess Muck had come. Before she left, the Goddess Muck suggested that one day they come on holiday to her. But when great Zeus said that she could count on it, and they would all descend on her quite soon, it put the poor goddess in an awful panic.

"I think, Lord Zeus," said the poor goddess, "that I

could only put up two of you at once. I have only for my residence a humble hill, but very welcome I will make you," she added hastily, fearful that her caution might be taken. for ingratitude.

And so the visit came about. It was the month of May when the goddess welcomed Zeus and his wife.

"So this is Great Britain!" cried the Olympian god. "How very small it is! My word, how glad we are we've found you. Your directions were perfect, my friend, or I'd never have discovered you amongst the tracts of land that lie between our countries. What wonderful clouds you have!" And Lord Zeus, the cloud gatherer as he was known back in ancient times, collected a good armful of English cloud and made himself extremely comfortable on what was known as the Beacon Hill where once the ancient Britons had lit fires to warn of imminent invasion. Perhaps they should have lit one now?

The ox-eyed, white-armed Hera presented gifts to the Goddess Muck:bowls wrought in gold and filled with Greek ambrosia; and fine stone jars of nectar. The Goddess Muck was overwhelmed by such show of generosity, and was greatly worried as to what she herself could give them in return.

Might her visitors expect a sacrifice of sheep or goats or a five-year bullock? If so they would be disappointed. The British guarded all their livestock with their lives. They never offered up burnt offerings as once the ancient Greeks had done to their immortals.

But Lord Zeus was on holiday! He cast his mighty gaze around the panoramic views, to the wooded slopes and gentle curves and undulating valleys. He seemed pleasantly surprised by all the herds of cattle and the flocks of sheep, and bent an ear favourably towards the lowing and the bleating which wafted gently upwards like the issuing of smoke from the mouths of cigarette smokers. And, as he looked with pleasure at the scenic views, he saw the farmer's wife come up the hill to see some twenty bullocks in a field. Her cattle dog ran on before her, putting up a pheasant from the hedge which, with a screech, flew off low across the fields.

Zeus spied the woman and was seized with a desire to speak to her. The Goddess Muck saw the mischief in his eyes and was dismayed – his reputation, she had heard, was bad where mortal women were concerned. In a great flap the poor goddess said:"Now that you have done me the honour of a visit, you must let me show you something of the British Isles."

Zeus smiled, his eyes sparkling, as he watched the farmer's wife. His queen knew very well the symptoms shown by her husband when some naughty plan had seized him.

"That woman down there,"Zeus said – he often liked to satisfy himself that Hera's jealousy could be aroused as easily as in centuries gone by – "who is she?"

The Goddess Muck lied a little. She told Lord Zeus that the woman was a good, devoted wife who helped her husband on the farm and that he depended on her;that the farmer was a brave and noble fellow born to the city but who had forfeited his city pleasures (and anxieties) for a life of stubborn toil upon the land. Thinking this brief biography would check his ardour, the goddess was alarmed to see that instead it further excited his interest.

"Tell me, Muck, what makes the woman look so woebegone? I have a great longing to see the woman smile."

"A blow has hit them on the farm," said the goddess. "A strange illness has struck down many calves."

"Ho, ho! Have they offended their great God?" cried Zeus. "What have they done to warrant such displeasure?"

"Here in the British Isles I think you'll find they'll seek a scientific reason for the illness," the Goddess Muck replied.

"What temerity! To offend against heaven and then pronounce the problem of ill-health a scientific one seems to me gross ignorance – or arrogance – or both!"

"It is quite true," answered the poor goddess, "that we can make them suffer for their sins by casting illness on their beasts, but I can assure you they will find a remedy! Each malady is found to have a cause, and so Jehovah's wrath is often thwarted by these modern, learned vets.Far better, in my view, to worry them with weather. That is something the poor British have not learned yet to control." And the Goddess Muck laughed merrily at the memory of her cruel revenge on the farmer who once failed to notice how much he owed to her goodwill and patronage in his early years of farming.

But now the farmer's wife was calling out aloud to heaven:"Oh, God!" she cried, "what have we done to deserve this illness in our little calves? I know I've done what I should not, and there are things I should have done which I have not, but have I been so bad that all our calves need die? Oh, save us from this terrible calamity!"

Zeus glanced at the Goddess Muck and remarked: "She doesn't seem to have much faith in science."

The Goddess Muck felt a little embarrassed for the woman, and said nervously:"She is praying just in case."

"In case of what, my friend?"

But the Goddess Muck said nothing in reply. Zeus laughed heartily. He told the goddess that it was a great comedy, and he certainly would not intervene. Although, he added, it would amuse him to pit his wits against the great almighty God who had usurped his own pre-eminence two thousand years ago. But no, he had come on holiday and, as a visitor, he would observe the customs of the British and not interfere in human or immortal matters. And Zeus' sparkling eyes fixed themselves once more on the farmer's wife who was bleating like a sheep and asking heaven for forgiveness for things past and in the future, and promising to go to church if all her calves were cured. All the way down the hill she could be heard, her voice gradually receding until she was swallowed up inside the house.

"What are their symptoms?" Zeus asked.

"They grind their teeth, lose their eyesight and blunder blindly in their shed. After a day or two they suffer cruel convulsions. Already four have died," the Goddess Muck explained. "The vet has diagnosed the illness comes from lead-paint poisoning, and yet they don't respond to treatment."

In vain the Goddess Muck tried to change the topic and spoke about the fine cities she would like to take her guests to see:the cathedrals and the castles, and all the scientific wonders of Great Britain. But Zeus persisted. "Now I am here, how can I gain access to the farmer's house?" he asked. "If I were to take on mortal guise arriving as a beggar at their door, would I be welcomed in and given room beside their hearth? Would I be fed and cared for by the farmer's wife?"

The Goddess Muck was quick to tell her guest that British women did not take kindly to a beggar at the door. Indeed, she told him, the British were suspicious of all beggars, believing them to be suffering from fleas and lice; far from a beggar turning out to be a prince or king or god, in their view a beggar was exactly what he seemed, a ne'er do well, a scrounger and a thief.

"Then how would you advise me to gain entry to the farmer's home?" asked Zeus.

"You could," said the poor Goddess Muck, who wished only to please her lordly guest, "pretend you were a student looking for hired labour for the silage and the hay-making."

But now Hera intervened:"You fickle husband! Why ask our friend Muck what you should do? You have never in the past found it a problem to ravage every woman whom you take a fancy to! Why talk about it when you know how angry it will make me!"

"Petulant woman!" Zeus grumbled, pleased to have aroused her jealousy once more. "Always trying to hold me to your will, for what your will is worth! Let our friend Muck take you off to see the city sights, whilst I rest here a while. The journey has been long and I am very comfortable reclining on this great British cloud."

His ox-eyed wife knew better than to fall in with this plan. "I think not, dear husband," she declared. "I too am much fatigued after our long journey." And for the time being nothing more was said about the farmer's wife, much to the Goddess Muck's relief.

Next day Dawn, to confound the British forecasters as was her wont, rose from her couch wearing a very pretty skirt of amber, flaming red and pink. The Goddess Muck woke early and was up and ready waiting for her guests. Glancing down towards the farm she saw a tall, fair haired youth greeting the farmer's wife. At first she thought it must be the foreign student who had been inadvertently delayed due to some dispute amongst disgruntled ferry workers. Then she remembered she had told Zeus how the farmer was expecting this student, a stranger to him. Looking down again she saw he had a god-like quality and immediately she was alarmed.

Hera, refreshed after a night's sleep, came down declaring she had never been so comfortable – such beds of cloud, she said. She was about to ask the Goddess Muck if she had seen her husband when she noted the poor goddess' confusion. At the same time she saw the tall, fair haired youth down in the farmyard speaking to the farmer's wife. She saw through the disguise at once. Oh treachery! With great presence of mind she hid her fury from the Goddess Muck.

"Dear friend," the ox-eyed goddess said, "I have an interest in agricultural matters and would so like to take back to my sister Demeter, goddess of corn, details of how people work their farms in Britain. Would you allow me to join the farmer and his wife – and that noble youth who seems now to have joined them despite the ferrymen's dispute (and she gritted her teeth as she said the words). "How would you advise me to get down amongst them?" she asked, smiling through the fumes of rage which flowed with every word.

The Goddess Muck was tactful in the extreme, so anxious was she that Queen Hera should keep the mighty Zeus from causing havoc on the farm. They understood each other perfectly. And so a plan was made.

Very soon there appeared riding along the high-banked Devon lanes, a young woman cyclist. Never had the local Gossips seen such cycling! What amazing power, one cried! What a cycle, cried another! Then they gasped, dismayed, as suddenly a cycle-wheel went flat, and the young woman flew over the handle-bars and lay in a heap on the roadside. The farmer passing on his tractor at that instant was aghast, and leapt down to assist the poor young woman.

The farmer's wife, when she saw this new disaster, cried: "Oh, God! another disaster! First the dying calves! Now a bleeding cyclist! Oh, never will I do wrong again!" And she ran, looking for the first-aid kit which, as usual when required, was nowhere to be found.

As soon as Queen Hera found the student alone with her, she opened her eyes and said: "You! How dare you, husband! How dare you behave towards me in this manner!"

Lord Zeus, caught in the act of his duplicity, braved it out before his wrathful wife. "You think you know me well, my queen, but I do assure you my interest in the farm is quite sincere."

His wife was not deceived. "It is too bad of you to lie to me like this! Three thousand years I've had of you and you never change! Remember we are here as visitors, and you and I both know it's only courtesy, while accepting hospitality, to refrain from muddling the affairs of those who welcome us. Have we not been told by poor Muck that the farmer and his wife live on a knife-edge between success and ruin?"

"To show you my sincerity, dear wife, I'll turn myself into a calf and eat nuts from a trough, if it will please you," Zeus replied, and so saying, in a trice he was one of fifteen in the shed of dying animals – a most comely bullock, strong-limbed, soft-muzzled, dewy-eyed with lashes long and slanting; his coat was rough and curly, and he had a strong and lively tail. The truth was that he knew the farmer's wife would soon be coming out to feed and fuss over her little calves.

And so the Zeus calf stood strong and healthy amongst

those others who, with grinding teeth and twitching bodies, held their heads high and blundered blindly round their shed, knocking into the stone walls. The farmer's wife noticed him at once, and was delighted by his health and vigour. She fondled his strong neck while he, in his turn, whisked his tail and sucked her fingers joyously. He was greedily devouring her bare arm when her attention was drawn from him to a fast car squealing to a standstill like a stuck pig in the yard. From it leapt the vet. "Vitamin B deficiency!" he shouted and, with a bottle of the antidote and a hypodermic needle, he hurried to the shed of dying animals.

A cock crowing on a dung-heap nearby drew Zeus' attention urgently. It was the Goddess Muck calling to him.

"Your disguise, immortal Zeus, is discovered. I fear you find my hospitality is lacking or you'd not have left my small and modest hill to find amusement elsewhere. I do beseech you come back with me now. I will give you what poor hospitality I can. I do beseech you, come back with me now! If you delay you will not enjoy what now the vet has come to do!" And the crowing cock screeched off, flapping its wings and disappeared into a thicket.

Zeus' zenith and omnipotence lay in a bygone age; he knew nothing of modern science. He was tempted to defy the Goddess Muck until he saw the vet and farmer swinging into action. Seizing each calf in turn they jabbed the struggling beast with a hypodermic needle in the rump. Immediately Zeus shrank and slid as a worm under the stable door to become the tall, fair-haired youth again. Now Hera, who had heard the Goddess Muck, touched his arm and whispered: "Let us not offend these lesser beings of divinity, my lord." And she drew almighty Zeus off. Once out of sight they whirled off, squabbling like two conflicting winds.

"Do what you like in your own country, but here remember your manners!" she urged. "I know you very well and find your deception of poor Muck thoughtless and unkind."

"Stop your infernal bickering, woman! I'll put it right with poor Muck, never fear!"

Back already on her hill, the Goddess Muck saw her two visitors appear. They smiled reassuringly at her and declared themselves fascinated by this small English farm.

"Great heavens, Muck, I wouldn't have missed my venture into mortal guise for all the world! I trust you didn't mind my taking that short visit down amongst them? This modern age of science is most interesting! And will the farmer's wife now go to church as I heard her promising her almighty God she would? Or will she pin the miracle of healing on the vet?" And he looked down towards the farm, and his eyes sparkled briefly as they rested on the woman. She was leaning on the stable door watching the young calves now rapidly recovering.He saw her scanning the small animals, looking for the young and joyous strong-limbed beast. He could see she was surprised it was no longer there, yet the numbers were correct. And then he saw her look around to find the tall, fair-haired youth, but could not see him either.

He drew his eyes away and relaxed comfortably pretending no more interest in the farm. "Great heavens, Muck!" he cried, "what a good holiday I'm having! What green fields you have in this fine land! What wonderful scenery you enjoy! What rivers and valleys! How we envy you your small domain, upon my word, we do!"

Such flattery! His words made the poor goddess

puff up with pride. She could feel the colour rise to her immortal cheeks. The white-armed Hera cast a glint-eyed look at her immortal huband, and then at the small Goddess Muck. She was reassured that the great Zeus was now nobly playing his part as a visitor to a foreign land. He was making up for any momentary distress he might have caused his hostess earlier.

For the time being all was well down on the farm.

A FARMER'S YFE

"There is no doubt that every farmer needs a yfe."

"A yfe? What is a yfe?"

"My dear man, don't you know what a yfe is? Why, it is an indispensable bit of equipment – a must for every farmer."

"Why? What does it do, this yfe?"

"What does it do? It does everything! Not only does it wash and clean inside the house, but it does everything the farmer grumbles loud and long about outside as well."

"Good heavens! give me a yfe, then! Where can I find a yfe? How does it function? Is it expensive to buy? Is it expensive to run? Is it complicated? Can it be easily understood? Tell me about this marvel of marvels!"

"My dear friend, one question at a time, please! What is a yfe? Well, a yfe is an object that stands on two legs. Make sure, when you acquire your yfe that it has two legs which operate, a yfe with one leg or a dicky leg should be absolutely rejected. Secondly, make certain the yfe has a head with a screw loose; a head screwed up will be absolutely infuriating to a farmer and might cause more trouble than it's worth. Thirdly, the yfe should have two arms as strong as the handles of a wheelbarrow. A yfe should be tested out for strength and durability by having it on trial. If, after a week, the yfe is found to be unable to bear a sack of cattle cake, or if its two strong legs give way beneath the burden of such weights then the yfe should be sent back and another one tried out. So – two strong, sturdy legs; two tough arms able to bear heavy burdens; and a screw loose in the head, and the farmer then can rest assured he has the best mechanical equipment he could wish for on his farm.

"Is it better than a tractor, then?"

"Better than a tractor? Good heavens! Would you bring a tractor in the house? And if you did what would it do? Nothing! No, no, a yfe is far superior to a tractor! Have you ever heard of a tractor washing out the farmer's dirty shirts and trousers?"

It's a sort of washing machine, then? Is a yfe some sort of apparatus that washes?"

"A washing machine? Some sort of washing apparatus? Oh, dear me! Have you ever seen a washing machine dart across a field to cut off cattle heading for an open gate? Have you? No. But a yfe will! A yfe will run like a hare on its two strong legs; and a yfe is often to be seen washing out a garment. A yfe does everything! It irons and folds and puts the clothes away in cupboards – each garment in the cupboard where it ought to go."

"A robot! The yfe is a robot?"

"No, no! The yfe is not a robot. A robot is not as versatile as a yfe! A robot will do so much and no more and must be programmed. No, a yfe is far superior to a robot. A yfe responds to the farmer's voice which is truly wonderful.

Give a farmer a yfe and if he treats the yfe reasonably (or even unreasonably) the yfe will do all manner of dull, objectionable chores no other implement would undertake, let alone a robot. Take an emergency on the farm: a yfe (believe it or not) will operate on instructions from the farmer using its arms or legs, even its head with the loose screw, to help the farmer accomplish some unpleasant task – a midnight calving, for example. The farmer will not hesitate to use the strong arms of this useful implement and make it haul with him to calve a cow. Then out again at dawn the yfe will go and fetch the cows, and it will milk them too. My word! give a farmer a good yfe and he will be sleeping in his bed, snoring, while the yfe does his work for him. But let me tell you, it need not be all work! A farmer can get pleasure from his yfe as well. It's not unusual to see a farmer dancing with his yfe."

"Dancing?"

"Oh, certainly. A farmer going to a dance will take his yfe. At a village dance the farmer will be seen doing a barn dance with his yfe, or with another farmer's yfe, come to that. It's true, sometimes, a farmer tries to steal another's yfe if he doesn't like his own, but in general farmers respect each other's property and hand the yfe back after having danced with it."

"I suppose a farmer knows that if he steals another's yfe the village will be up in arms?"

"Oh, no doubt about that at all. Besides, the farmer's children (if he has any) get used to the same yfe about the place. Yes, this amazing piece of machinery bears with the farmer's children too. Never mind how frightful are the little brats, the yfe will suffer them. It might even deliver a well-aimed blow to the backside of a son or daughter, but not before that child deserves it. More often, though, a child is seen with its arms around the yfe, even kissing it, which is amazing. And the yfe will be often seen at the wheel of the farmer's car, driving it and taking the farmer's children back and forth from school. In fact, the yfe is so highly thought of that the head master of the school will be seen taking aside the yfe and speaking to it, as if the yfe had the ability to make the child work harder or behave with more respect – truly remarkable, wouldn't you agree?"

"It seems a yfe is everywhere at once?"

"That is very true. If the farmer has anything to complain of it will be that he may not find his yfe where he last saw it."

"If a yfe can even drive the car then there's no knowing where the yfe might be! Surely, the farmer worries that his yfe, this undefinable piece of equipment, might drive his precious car into a ditch?"

"Funny you should say that! The odd thing is the farmer when he sits inside the car and the yfe is at the wheel often yells or shows extreme anxiety – not that the yfe is deflected from its task one jot – no, the yfe will keep on driving come what may. But the farmer, showing so little trust in how the yfe drives the car with him in it, shows no anxiety whatsoever when allowing his yfe to take his children off to school and back again each day. A little odd, wouldn't you agree?"

"Very peculiar, yes. And does a yfe drive a tractor too?"

"A good yfe will get on to a tractor too and drive it, oh, yes, most certainly it will. A yfe, taken on trial, should be mounted on a tractor straight away. A yfe can be relied upon to harrow, roll, fertilise, cut grass, ted or bale the hay. Of course, there is the problem that a yfe can only do one job at a time. So that if a farmer sets his yfe to cut a field of hay he'll find he has no supper and the children will be left at school, or his calves are not attended to. So then he himself will have to cook, which, of course, no farmer ever likes to do."

"But how is this yfe powered? Does it run on electricity? Does it have to be plugged into a socket?"

"Electricity! a socket! No, no! There's no electricity involved!"

"Batteries, then? Does it need batteries? Or does it run on petrol or diesel, perhaps?"

"No, no, forget the use of fuel! The most amazing thing about a yfe – and really the most convenient – is that it runs on boiled eggs, soup, bread and cheese and meat and vegetables."

"Great heavens! It costs no more than an ordinary daily ration of food?"

"That's right. It costs as little as a man's dinner to run it, and it does everything needing to be done in return."

"Amazing. It costs less than a tractor to run and does much more? But I can't believe it's only soup that drives it?"

"Well, I have heard say that a yfe has batteries that need to be recharged, but I've yet to see them. If it falters, then the farmer would be wise to rest it for a while. One night will suffice, and in the morning it will be ready for action, as good as new again."

"You don't say!"

"It's surprising how little goes wrong with a yfe compared, say, to a tractor. A thirty-year-old tractor may not always start – it may have to be run downhill to get it going – not so a yfe! If a yfe seems uncooperative at all then a good shout from the farmer (or a soft word even) and the yfe will soon be on its two strong legs again."

"But these batteries, where are they to be found?"

"In-built, my friend. Nothing to worry about. The less you tamper with the inner workings of a yfe the better. If it has been overworked then just let it rest a while. You might try giving it some food – bread and cheese, or something."

"You don't need to take it apart and oil it or anything?"

"No, no. Just let it be. That is the joy of a yfe. Unlike all other farm machinery it is as good as new at thirty, forty, fifty, sixty even. In fact, it could be said that it improves with age. Better still, knock a yfe and it does not dent; and if it tears it will repair itself with the minimum of fuss. Very seldom does a yfe break down. But if it does the farmer will be well advised to ask himself what he has done to make his yfe crack up. It's up to the farmer to keep an eye on it. A yfe will serve him well only if he treats it with respect – with love even."

"Certainly I'd love my yfe if I was fortunate enough to have a good one. But tell me, how much does it cost, this yfe? It must be beyond the means of any but the richest farmer."

"Good heavens no! The wonder of a yfe is that it costs nothing to acquire."

"What? Did you say nothing?"

"Nothing."

"You mean it's bought on – well, a credit card?"

"No, no, nothing so crude."

"Buy now and pay later? Is that what you mean?"

"A yfe is never bought – well, a few free gifts can acquire a wife of course, but – "

"You mean it's on loan to the farmer?"

"No. Once he has decided on his yfe the farmer merely has the formality of declaring that his yfe is his for better or for worse and he promises to cherish it forever – only a formality, you understand, no farmer takes it seriously.

Take, for example, the other declaration that he makes: he promises to hand all his worldly goods over to the yfe, which, of course, he never does, but it is well worth his while to make the declaration in order to acquire the yfe."

"Oh, well worth while!"

"And while we're on the subject of money, let me tell you this: thanks to his yfe the farmer pays less tax! Yes! He can write into his farm accounts the fact that his yfe costs him a hefty sum of money every year. It's written down as labour, though, of course, the money's never moved from his account. Who'd ever think of handing money over to a yfe? My dear man, the idea is preposterous, a joke! Imagine a yfe with money? What would it do with it? Can you see the farmer taking his yfe off to the shops to spend his money? Would he be happy on the farm thinking that his yfe had taken off his car and driven off to town with a large sum of his money which he knows (and so does his accountant as also does his bank manager) he needs in order to buy animals or another tractor or some fertilizer, cattle cake, or to erect another building – no, the idea's preposterous!

No, the farmer has his money for the farm! His yfe functions very well without it! That is the beauty of the farmer's yfe."

"Truly remarkable!"

"Oh, yes. No other piece of equipment or machinery is of such benefit to the farmer. It is very seldom that a farmer's yfe is given up as useless, too much can be got out of the worst and such a great deal can be got out of the best. Like a shovel, every farmer needs one. It is with good reason – and this shows their true excellence – that if a farmer loses one, heaven forbid! but if he loses one, the first thing that he does is to look out for another. Absolutely no farmer would dream of continuing his livelihood without a yfe to help him…"

"Remarkable."

"Yes, truly remarkable!"

HUNTING HUMANS

One winter's morning when a freezing mist hung about the woods and fields, a herd of cows in steamy warmth lay placidly on straw inside their shed. Their ruminations and.comfortable regurgitations would have continued unabated had not the cry of a hunstsman and the sound of a hunting horn from a nearby wood disturbed the peace.

A couple of cows eating in the yard outside withdrew their heads from their feeding ring and turned in time to see a russet fox streak across the frosted field up the hill behind their winter quarters. From a coppice came the odd yodelling of hounds, then several together and then suddenly the whole wood was alive with the concerted baying of the pack as they broke from the trees and, with their noses to the ground, pursued the fox which had by now vanished. Down.the lane skirting the wood was heard the heavy tread of horses. They passed through an open gate and were soon going at full gallop carrying their mounts. The two cows in the yard watched the scene. It wasn't often that their dull lives were presented with a spectacle like this.

"Why can't we have fun like that?" said one of them.

The word was passed around the herd and a few idly raised their heads whilst others lumbered to their feet. All agreed that a bit of sport would be amusing for a change.

When next the farmer came into their yard and began forking up some sodden silage into a wheelbarrow, he heard a cow address him:"Master, we have seen the hunt and we ourselves would like permission to go hunting too one day."

The farmer, who was quite used to communing with his. cows due to the isolation of the farm, replied reasonably:"A day's hunting, hm? Well, we'll see."

"We only wish to do what we've seen men do," said Buttercup, a placid favourite of the farmer.

"Well, if men do it, there's no reason why you shouldn't too, if you are able,"said the farmer, humouring his animals and dismissing the thought as of no consequence as they were only cows.

Soon Ethel, self nominated ring-leader, stepped forward. She had a vicious temper and, as she stood before him, her breath blew in bursts from her nostrils into the cold air like a dragon breathing fire. "You must promise us!" she said.

By now many of the cows had left the shed and were drawing near. Their breath seemed to boil around the farmer who with his dung-fork was picking up the semi-frozen sodden silage and heaping it into his wheelbarrow. "Promise!" The word seemed to insinuate itself into the farmer's mind.

"Darned animals! Get out of my way, the lot of you!"

"Promise!"

"If it'll keep you happy, then I promise!" And he picked

up the handles of his wheelbarrow and prepared to leave. But Ethel stood before him.

"We will want a pack of dogs," she said.

"Out of my way, you!" And the farmer put down his barrow preparing to whack her rump. Ethel remained sideways on, her head turned defiantly as she snorted breath out of her nostrils.

"So it's a pack of dogs you're after, is it? All right, a pack of dogs it is," agreed the farmer.

"And all doors must be locked," continued Ethel. "All farmers must be in the fields."

Buttercup tried to nuzzle him. "Get off me, you old fool," the farmer said.

"We intend to hunt every human that we see," said Ethel, and a bit of white of eye like a crescent moon glinted menacingly. The farmer stood rooted to the ground uncertain if he had heard correctly. "We intend to hunt and kill just as you humans do," said Ethel staring him full in the face. The words 'you promised' were repeated in chorus as the other cows gathered around him.

The farmer's mind worked fast. To back down from this foolish promise would bring down on him a multitude of problems. Angry, discontented cows would bring him to eventual bankruptcy, that was certain. Times were hard enough. Vicious words from Ethel broke in on his thoughts.

"Just as you stop the earths of foxes so they cannot return into them, so we will lock the doors of all your houses so that you cannot escape from us by running back into your homes."

"That's right!" cried all the cows together.

"And if you cannot run fast enough then the hounds will kill you!" said Ethel, the crescent moon in her eye waxing more menacingly than ever. "We've heard it said it is quite painless being torn limb from limb. We've heard it said it's better to be chased and killed than to be shot or gassed in your own home. It's what we've heard men say about hunting." And she continued with malicious.glee: "We would like to hunt on a regular basis, once a week throughout the winter."

"Like men do – just like men," said Buttercup placidly, flicking her tail.

"Just one hunt will be one too many," said the farmer grimly.

The bulk of all the cows gathering around him reminded him how much he had to fear his animals who, by the nature of their size were very much superior in weight and strength to humans. Somehow he must pit his wits against these foolish beasts. He heard Ethel screaming abuse at him:"You are killers all of you! You exterminate everything you have a mind to!" The whites of her eyes were now three-quarter moons. The farmer privately decided he would cull her from the herd as soon as possible. She had always been troublesome. Indeed, he had lost a front tooth by her viciously kicking when he was placing the milking cluster on her teats. At the time he had given her the benefit of the doubt, feeling sympathy at how painful it must be to be milked after being newly calved when the udder was swollen tight with milk. Pain! This gave him an idea.

By now all the cows had taken up the cry:"We live under your rule and know nothing of what it is to feel free. All we know is fear. Fear that if we do not produce milk to the very pint that you demand you will send us to the extermination yards. You are murderers all of you! If you do not yourselves kill by strangling chickens and shooting pheasant, then you use others to kill for you – cats to kill mice and rats and moles; terriers to kill hares and otters and badgers! the things that we endure, it's horrible! Revenge, revenge, revenge!" they cried, their ears laid back with fanatical loathing.

The farmer realized that his situation was perilous. Extreme ingenuity was called for if he and his family were to survive.

"You think it is any easier to be human?" he demanded. "You think I am freer than you? Do you realize that if I did not care for you you would not be alive now?"

"You think?" screamed Ethel.

"Quite decidely not,," the farmer replied.

"Try us, then!"

"Very well. But first let's fix the day for your hunt," the farmer said reasonably. "Perhaps, as I am to be hunted, you'll be good enough to let me name the day?"

The cows consulted together and then said:"You may name it, but it must be within a week."

"All right", the farmer answered. In seven days you may have your hunt. Until then you fend for yourselves, so there!" And the farmer turned on his heel, throwing down his dung fork and casting aside his overalls. He marched down to the house where he found his wife preparing his lunch. She looked up as he entered the kitchen.

"Drop all that," the farmer said in a voice she had never heard him use before. "We are taking a week's holiday."

The farmer's wife was amazed. "A holiday? But – but what about the animals?"

"Let them fend for themselves!"

"But what's happened?" his wife demanded, removing her apron.

"What's happened?" he exploded, "this is what's

happened!" And he related to her all that had passed between him and his cows. As he told her he steered her up the stairs, got down the suitcases and packed the clothes they needed for their holiday.

The animals watched from their yard as they saw the car back out of the garage. As he drove away the farmer did not once glance in their direction which was very odd; usually he cast an eye up the yard to check that all was well; usually they were never out of his mind which, although comforting to them, was also irritating and caused them to defy him on occasions if only to show him that they had minds of their own.

As the car drove off the entire herd bellowed with joy. At last they were left to their own devices! They were at long last able to fend for themselves and each one of them believed implicitly that she had the capacity to get out and eat as much winter fodder as she possibly could. It was wonderful! They gathered round the bale of silage in the feeding ring and each had a bellyful.

That evening there was no milking. The cows collected in their shed and lay down, eyeing each other dubiously. Ethel was not going to admit that her udder was bursting with milk and she was painfully uncomfortable. She lay in an ungainly attitude, her udder splayed out sideways with milk spurting from each teat leaving little pools of milk. Other cows were hanging their heads through the bars of the feeding ring searching for the last of the silage, aware that their rumbling stomachs were empty and there was nothing more to be had. Worst of all, there was a hard frost that night and, when the cows came to drink, they found their water frozen. They eyed each other silently and chewed the cud over and over and over again, silently pondering the possible outcome to what already seemed an appalling situation.

Two days later, with no fodder and no water and their yard sodden with excrement, they were really worried. Ethel by now was suffering extreme pain and discomfort. It was clear that she needed antibiotics because she had developed an infection in her udder – mastitis it was called. Worse still the cows could hear their little calves calling to them. They too were.not being fed. The cows called back, but none of them could open the gate to get out. Oh, if only they had human qualities! If only they had the ability to feed and milk themselves, then all would be well! They were in a terrible plight and were growing weaker and weaker by the hour. Ethel's temperature was up and she was lying on her side, her legs rising in the air which was always a bad sign as it brought pressure on the heart and inevitable death. The others were also beginning to lie flat out, neck and head extended in abject misery, hearing their poor calves weakly calling to them for food. They no longer cared about life, they were ready to die. Yes, yes, men were best! They should never have thought that they could compete with men!

Suddenly, as they lay drowning in melancholy, they heard the farmer's car in the yard. Normally they would have brought their ears forward contentedly, knowing that the farmer had returned and some attention would be coming their way. But now they lay exhausted, without energy enough to flick an ear.

A moment later the farmer and his wife came up to see them. "Well?" cried the farmer, "look at you all! Not three days have passed and you are near to death from the look of.you! You poor, helpless monsters! Do you want to hunt and kill men still? What? You don't answer! Speak up! Do you or don't you want to hunt and kill us?"

Ethel with a bitter struggle attempted to rise, but succeeded only in floundering and getting herself further wedged beneath a metal bar which partitioned off her cubicle.

"Help us, master," she whispered. And from all around the cowshed came the same sounds of distress as all implored him to help.

"Very well," the farmer said with satisfaction. "I will help you but on one condition." The murmur that came from all the prostrate cows reassured the farmer that they consented. "I will help you only if you promise me that you will never, ever again demand to hunt us farmers. Kill us and this will be your fate." Even as he spoke he cut the binder twine on a bale of sweet smelling hay and walked along the rows of recumbent animals and gave each a handful. As they curled their tongues around this fodder they could hear the farmer's wife breaking the ice on their water trough. Life began to surge back into them. With joy they heard the milking parlour engine start. Each animal in turn struggled to her feet. Ethel somehow was helped up. The farmer gently relieved her swollen udder where she stood. The relief was unimaginable.

"Do you promise?" asked the farmer.

"We promise," Ethel said and even turned her head as the farmer relieved her bursting udder. ."We're sorry. We know we really do depend on your fine judgement, master. I will give you more milk in the future and will never kick you in the face again." With sickening subservience she then asked:"Did you have a nice holiday, master?"

"Hum!" the farmer grunted. He did not really like this change of attitude in the animal. He never had trusted her and did not trust this polite concern for him. "To be frank, I was too worried over you darned cows to enjoy it," he said. A gleam of pleasure showed itself in Ethel's eye. She half raised a hind leg but put it down again. It might seem that their welfare depended on the farmer, but it seemed too that the farmer's welfare depended on them. He was in their power as much as they were in his. She gave a deep bellied burp and began to chew the matter over. If she chewed long and hard enough she would surely come up with some solution? So she started ruminating, but went on chewing for so long that eventually she forgot what the problem was. She only knew that she felt better and they would willingly forego their day of hunting for such quiet contentment.

A FLOCK OF TOURISTS

The natural habitat of tourists is the beach and in the summer these beasts are to be seen in droves all along the coasts of Britain. At about five or six o'clock each evening all tourists will be seen legging it away from the sands in search of their night's shelter.

As a cash crop they are to be recommended to supplement a farmer's income. They have their season coming with the summer and going with the winter. They are never 'finished off' at farms but a profit from these curious beasts is possible if they are carefully handled and adequately fed.

It should always be remembered that tourists are not on the farm in order to be looked at and admired like Jacob sheep but are there like sheep to be politely fleeced. On no account, however, should a farmer's wife fling them to the ground, turn them on their backs to fleece them.

No, to fleece tourists she should smile at them and keep smiling even though her jaw stiffens, until they willingly withdraw from their persons a wallet or a purse (males have wallets and females have purses), which is the only recognisable sexual difference on a cold English summer's day when their bodies are encased in wool.

A farmer's wife undertaking the task of keeping tourists should not do it lightly. Her duties will entail feeding and watering them daily and providing them with suitable sleeping quarters – always with fresh bedding for each new arrival; to skim over such trivial details will reduce the profit margin as the beasts will be heard grumbling and will not thrive – indeed, will not return after their first visit to the beach.

Those with young at foot will need extra attention and should be watched over eagle-eyed. Infants of single suckling tourists present little problem, but small tourists gambolling like lambs will not discriminate between what they gambol into or over and may be destructive. Extra penning is to be recommended, or yards or fields in which such frolicsome creatures can run free. For a farmer's wife to raise her voice or whack a toddling tourist may well cause the tourist dam to clutch her small offspring and disappear without trace. To have no tourist and no profit because the animal has gone is not good business.

Tourists thrive best on routine. During the day they will disappear but always return before dark to be fed and sheltered for the night. In general they are clean beasts and like things to be spotless. Their eating bowls and drinking troughs must be well washed after every meal and their quarters free from contamination such as the entrails of mice left by the cat, or the webs of spiders. Dirt makes them gather themselves together for a quick getaway which does not make for a good profitable business. It should be remembered that a tourist beast falling ill due to unhygienic conditions will bring some ministry or another down on the farmer like a load of hay or a ton of breeze blocks.

Tourists are not unlike cows in their eating habits, needing to be fed morning and night and often to be seen chewing like cows between meals. Unlike cows, however, the farmer's wife does not in any way want her tourists to give birth on the farm. It would be considered against ministry regulations for a tourist to produce her young on the farm. A pregnant tourist, imminently expectant, should not be taken in. Neither is it to be recommended that the farmer's wife should take in the very frail who, if the vet should see them would recommend that they should be put out of their misery. Faced with such creatures, however, the farmer's wife should not comment on their age as they hobble breathlessly about, neither should she help them as she would an ailing calf by heaving them to their feet, giving them a rough massage to help their circulation. Rather, she should treat them with the utmost care to get a profit from them before seeing them depart alive. Whatever happens they must not be allowed to expire on the farm or the authorities will start investigations which might prove quite unpleasant.

Some tourists will come to the farm only for the mating. This occurs in private and no help is needed. Such tourists, never mind the weather, will hide themselves away in their sleeping quarters coming out only to be fed. When they are seen they wander everywhere entwined. Never try to come between them or they might turn nasty. They can be very pretty to look at. Apart from coming out to be fed they mostly hide themselves. Fortunately there is no mating cry such as occurs with the fox, the cat or a frustrated bitch.

A farmer's wife taking in tourists should be prepared

for the odd beast that smells of liquor. Such a one will arrive with eyes blurred, an unhealthy colour and with a weaving gait and a cry of 'gin-gin'. Faced with such a tourist it is wise to smile, even if it freezes on the face. Place a glass and a bottle of gin (smiling) before the creature and let it drink until it is legless. Fleece it as soon as possible and then next day pass the tourist on to another farm. If the cry is 'whisssshhhhkeeee' the treatment should be the same.

Some tourists like refreshment first thing in the morning. It is advisable to pander to such animals and let them have what they require. Such tourists will be found hiding themselves beneath their bedding with only their heads poking out. On seeing the farmer's wife they may well grunt, roll over, sigh, cough revoltingly, but pay no attention. Just lay the refreshment conveniently nearby and smile if it seems appropriate, but not if there is something to smile about, and then retreat quickly. Within the hour (unless it is a mating pair) the tourists will come for their food looking quite unlike the creatures that were seen asleep.

If the farmer's wife wants to make extra cash then she should prepare the evening meals for her tourists. If this is the case she should be prepared to take time and energy and thought in producing varied meals for them. Tourists never like left-overs, pig-swill or boiled up cabbage stalks. They will eat a meal fit for a peasant but ideally thrive best on wholesome, well cooked farm fare, not too rich nor too poor. The farmer's wife must be careful not to spend more on tourist food than she gets back. She would do well to consider whether to contract the work out to local specialists in the field of tourist meals. On the other hand, clever management and cunning rehashing of left-overs well disguised can produce the profit she is looking for.

A farmer's wife should always smile – it is part of good tourist keeping. A smile and a rehashed meal that tourists toy with rather than eat will bring that profit, whereas a grumpy scowl adds to the general stress and a profit may well turn into a loss. If the tourist begins to show signs of bad temper, food fad or fatulence, ignore the symptoms but keep smiling and the tourist will recover soon enough with luck.

The farmer's wife should allow time for tourist chatter too. The most demanding time from tourists is after feeding time in the evening when they are replete (when the farmer's wife herself is hungry). It is at this time that tourists like to chatter. When the farmer's wife is standing with a full tray in her hands, this is the signal for them to start. They may chatter for an hour without pause at the sight of the farmer's wife holding a full tray. The farmer's wife should stand there smiling, though her back is breaking and her legs are killing her, because by doing so she can expect (she may not get, but she can hope to get) that greater profit.

As yet an untapped market, but one that might prove more profitable than all previously tried tourist enterprises, is to tend and feed tourists until they are nicely plump. Then, always smiling, finish them off on the farm – never mind any ministry enquiry as the tourists won't be found. It is especially to be recommended in these hard times when farmers are told to turn their attention to new and profitable enterprises concerning anything but the old-fashioned notion of keeping pigs or sheep or milking cows. It would bring to the words 'tourist package holiday' a whole new meaning, and give the farmer's wife much more to smile about. Instead of supermarkets being overcrowded with tourists pushing trolleys there would be less of them pushing and more of them in the trolleys stamped with the flag of the country from which they came. Best of all the farmer's wife would have much more to smile about tending her flock of tourists because there would be the profit gained from tending them, and that further profit from packaging them.

THE BATTLE OF THE COWSHED

Words! Men are the victims of them! Men are the dupes, the pawns, the puppets of these small, ethereal creatures. It isn't men who make themselves dictators, words do; nor men who make themselves out stupid, only words. Look at politicians! Look at reporters, at writers, academics, lawyers! What are they all? The prisoners of words! They are what words have made them; they are their slaves!

What is history? Nothing but words. What is philosophy? Words. Theology? Words. What is an 'enemy'? What are 'commands'? All words! It is because of words men kill each other. No man would risk his life if words did not force him to it; if words did not stir him into action, did not seize him by the scruff and launch him into battle.

This is a tale of how words used the farmer and his wife. How words lured them from their city life and placed them in a rustic setting. How Gossip came into the neighbourhood and pumped the local jaws so that words flowed; how Gossip turned the people this way and then that to spot the farmer and his wife, and then the farmer's wife with someone else, and then the farmer too and – But that is the story of 'The Battle of the Cowshed'....

So to begin –

The word Beef occupied the farmer's mind like a great conqueror. Into the fields came bullocks, steers and heifers. For several weeks the farmer's wife, booted and anoraked, aproned and scarfed, stood by her husband, cold but loyal in the autumn mists, the wind and rain. She fed small calves, mixed milk, scattered straw, distributed hay. Loyalty and Devotion wrapped themselves about her and made her out a willing slave – for the time being anyway.

One day the farmer's wife was disturbed by a number of small Question Marks. These Question Marks came dancing by, gyrating gracefully and pirouetting elegantly on their toes before her. Each one begged an answer: would the cattle cease to graze if she pursued some other occupation? Could the farmer not take nails and staples from a paper bag instead of from her hand? Could her place in lanes and open gateways not be taken by a gate or hurdle? If the farmer wanted something living and companionable why not the cattle dog instead of her?

The Question Marks danced and pirouetted before her until quite suddenly Scholarship arrived and laid a grave hand on her brow and took her off indoors to study Greek. And now words harried her, all shapes and sizes of them: long ones, short ones, English ones and Greek ones, modern ones and ancient ones, all demanded her attention. And when they tired of being read in print like soldiers on parade, or of propagating themselves magically from the end of her pen, then they slid into her mind and amused themselves like children racing round a playground.

And while she grappled with these words indoors the

farmer went about his business outside. Determination clung to his head like a large sombrero hat. Thanks to Determination the farmer could easily unload ten tons of fertilizer bags, followed by two tons of cattle-cake, followed by a thousand land drains – all this without the least fatigue. As easily, with Scholarship's assistance, the farmer's wife could write ten thousand words, read the titles of two tons of books, learn fifty words in Greek and cover several miles of print, and show no sign of strain at all. And so time passed.

But while they were thus occupied there came into the neighbourhood a diplomat, an old and trusted friend of Passion, who was at this time on a long vacation having been shot in the leg by a Middle Eastern terrorist.

The wife of the diplomat hated Passion; Prude was her constant companion; and Prude often drew her compressed lips and gaunt figure in the image of her own likeness.

Because of his wife's aversion and the diplomat's enjoyment of him, Passion sometimes took his friend beyond the reaches of his home – which was understandable enough.

One day the diplomat felt Passion urging him to fresh adventures and so, without delay, he went limping to the library to exchange his books for others more appropriate to his present mood. Expectation and Ecstasy flew before him like two outriders drawing him along. He limped after them elegantly with the aid of a stout walking-stick; and everywhere he went eyes followed him: he always looked a diplomat amongst the rabble mob.

At the library, at the sound of a stout stick striking the floor boards, the farmer's wife looked up from her Greek lexicon and saw the diplomat. At the sight of the Greek lexicon open on the library table the diplomat looked down and saw the farmer's wife. He found a seat nearby, opened his book and fixed his eyes to the text. Expectation and Ecstasy flew back and forth between them creating a strong magnetic pull. But the diplomat was not a diplomat for nothing; although he knew at once that he was destined, he appeared only to be studying his book. Similarly, the farmer's wife, aware of the elegant addition to the readers in the room, continued to copy out her alpha, beta, gamma, delta as though nothing else interested her.

In time they met – not in the library as might have been supposed but, as it seemed by chance out hunting. Scholarship, growing weary one day, allowed Diversion to take the farmer's wife out following the hounds on foot. And there she saw the sporting diplomat leaning on his stick with his binoculars lifted to his eyes. A mutual friend, seeing each glancing at the other, soon introduced them both.

And Gossip was out hunting too. Yes, Gossip glanced at Passion toying with the diplomat; and Gossip saw how Pleasure lit the object of his eye and made her glow. And Gossip turned the locals all about and made them play the game of 'Spot the Diplomat and farmer's wife'.

And all the while the farmer was at work. Beneath the large sombrero of Determination, the farmer drove his pick into the ground to find blocked drains; and drove it in again to search for leaking water-pipes in fields. He drove his spade into the earth to dig out ditches, and drove in fencing stakes and gate posts. And when he wasn't driving things like that he drove in nails or drove the tractor or drove cattle from one pasture to another helped by his faithful cattle dog. And every evening Determination sat him down and kept him busy with his bills although he seldom paid them: he merely shuffled them and looked at them. Sometimes he added them all up and gulped before he shuffled them some more.

And every evening now the farmer's wife spoke Greek to him and he talked Beef back at her. To be blunt neither listened to the other. And so the farmer never heard her say she'd met a diplomat, nor she that he had dug two holes to find a leaking water pipe. He never heard her tell him she'd seen him in the library first and met him later at the local meet; nor did she hear the farmer say he'd found the pipe at last and cut and fitted a new joint. Nor did the farmer hear her tell him that a mutual friend had introduced them both and now had asked them out to dine; nor did she hear the farmer say that he had found another swamp and this must mean another leak and it must be a rotten pipe.

And so it came about that not long afterwards the farmer and his wife, the diplomat and his wife too, and several other agricultural people, found themselves by candle-light around the dinner-table.

And while the others spoke of rats and mice and moles and blight; of foxes, fences, riding, falling, good and bad weather, the diplomat (seated to the right of the farmer's wife) sat sleek and suave, and spoke of elegance and anarchy, of columns, domes and temples; of the Aegean sea and highjackers and terrorists. Passion played about the features of this sporting diplomat and drew the face of the farmer's wife towards him. And, as the meal progressed and the wine warmed and animated them, they never heard the others speak of cows and sheep, of digging holes and mending leaks in water pipes; of high market prices and low ones; of dead animals and live ones, and vet bills; but only what they themselves discussed such as the merits of a bygone age; of modern times and drama; of art and exhibitions; of opera and books. And Passion drew the head of the farmer's wife a shade nearer still.

But then something happened to cast a shadow over the party. The diplomat's wife, whose thin lips were being held compressed by Prude, was visited by Jealousy. Yes, there was Jealousy whose horrid light cast a green glow into the woman's eyes. And Jealousy made her two green eyes, like two round saucers, stare at the diplomat and farmer's wife until Etiquette intervened and made the woman turn to her companion on her left. Soon she too was chatting about autumn leaves and summer flowers; of cattle dogs, terriers, fleas and worming powders; of warble fly and drenches; of barley beef and mangel-wurzels. And the diplomat turned to his companion on his right and spoke of acreage and arable; of hounds and hunting, foxes and pheasants; of rat poison and seed potatoes. And so long as they both talked to their neighbours on the other side Jealousy receded, only to be seen when they turned towards each other once again.

And so the evening passed. The wife of the diplomat was first to leave, pleading her husband's bullet ridden leg as the excuse to go home early (doctor's orders she explained). Always the diplomat her husband did not demur but limped off after her, gracefully leaning on his stick. But then, you see, he'd gleaned some information: every Tuesday, he now knew, the farmer went to market leaving his wife at home, and he nestled this small piece of information secretly against his heart. Yes, he nestled it comfortably in his breast.

Next day the farmer's bank statement came through the post (he and his wife had a joint account). At once Anxiety seized him, and he accused his wife of profligacy which made her break two plates whilst washing up. Words such as Irresponsible and Extravagance flew from his mouth and struck her hard like rubber bullets. She stuttered like a stengun in response and pointed out he got the bills, not her. When did she ever buy calf nuts or cattle cake, gadgets or machinery, she demanded? Wasn't he the one who bought in calves and bought dried milk, fertilizer bags and hurdles, buckets, drain pipes, nails and tractor tyres and pitchforks, spades and shovels? Why blame her when all she did was read or write or study Greek? She never spent a thing, she said.

Determination sat round and unflappable on the farmer's head while his wife voiced this opinion. But Anxiety made him speak again. He pointed out that what he did was for the good of both of them and what she did was not; to which she at once retorted that she did the housework and carried out many small requests at inconvenient moments, like any servile half-besotted slave; and she only studied Greek when all this work was done. Yes, she would like to go to Greece, she said, to visit Delphi, Corinth and of course to see the Parthenon; but had she bought a ticket yet? No, she had not.

But Anxiety made the farmer now produce a carrier bag from which he drew an invoice and he asked her for an explanation. She nearly broke another plate. That, she told him, was for the dress she'd bought to wear the night before. She had, she said, told him about it; she had, she said, even worn it; she'd even asked him if he'd liked it; but he had been so taken up with water pipes and leaks and drinking troughs, punctures, diesel oil and anti-freeze that he hadn't heard a word she'd said or seen what she'd been wearing. The farmer thumbed the cheque-book stubs and turned up several further purchases which made him choke as though he'd swallowed several fish-bones. All his wife said then was that she'd thoroughly enjoyed the dinner and feeling elegant for once and hang the expense!

Now there was in the neighbourhood a blonde of great allure, a friend of the farmer's wife. This blonde would sometimes come up to the farm to see her friend but, finding her not there, she'd help the farmer with his work instead. She was a girl just bursting with Enthusiasm. She loved farms, loved animals, loved tractors and mechanical diggers and anything that needed to be fed or oiled. It was Enthusiasm brought her up and the farmer liked Enthusiasm.

The following Tuesday (market day) the blonde of great allure (Enthusiasm being what it was) asked if she could hitch a lift to town riding in the cattle lorry. The farmer readily agreed, believing she could help him load and unload two fat bullocks which he hoped to sell. But as they set off on the road together, who should occupy their persons in the cab but three bad words. These words at first pretended to be Friendship, Trust and good Sense; but no sooner were they on their way but they threw off their disguise and showed themselves for what they really were: Thrill, Ogle and Seduction. And all the way to market the three bad words teased and played about the farmer and the blonde, making them experience very pleasurable sensations.

Meanwhile the diplomat was coming to the farm; he did not feel his bullet wound at all so much was Passion playing with his thoughts. And flying along with him came Sin who, being only three letters, could easily slip into the minds of mortals.

The farmer's wife was in the yard when the diplomat arrived. She had been feeding calves and he relieved her of a bucket and pressed a book into her hands – a book on ancient Greece, a book he thought she'd like. And so she took him in and sat him down and stuck her nose into the book and asked all sorts of boring things about the marvels of that distant age, things far removed from the more pressing problems of the moment.

The diplomat sat gallantly nearby while Passion sent sparks flying from his eyes. But Sin, having no patience with such scholarly pursuits, soon dived from the head of the diplomat into the deep waters of the female mind, sending ever widening circles of meaning into her expression until the poor woman quite forgot what she was saying.

The diplomat was expert at such times. He recognized the signs at once, and gave himself up to the occasion. With a knowing smile he left his seat, dropped his stick and advanced like Zeus in a shower of gold to capture Danae.

And now Time flew – sometimes that happens: Time, contrary to human wishes, flies, while on occasions when Time would only fly, then Time stands still. But now Time flew and the farmer and the blonde were already driving back from market. Enthusiasm had caught them both and Determination was nowhere to be seen. And all the while the three bad words were playing wickedly about them.

As the farmer turned into the driveway he saw an unfamiliar car, muttered "damned visitor!" and drove on up to the top yard to keep out of the way. There he embraced the blonde and, urged on by the three bad words, he embraced her once again and led her to the cowshed.

Now Trouble came. He always lurked about where management was slacking off and, it has to be admitted that the farmer and his wife were both preoccupied with matters far from agricultural at that time. So Trouble came and, seeing two untied hurdles in the yard, he urged some bullocks past them into the big-bagged silage. Once there they tore the heavy-duty plastic with their teeth, climbed the bags and ravaged every one of them. Up came the cattle dog snapping at their tails and Trouble, like a great egg-whisk, whipped them all up until they were a frenzied whirl of hooves, split bags, mud, slurry, flying fur and teeth. Over went the hurdles and the bullocks, with their tails aloft, broke from the yard and away, away, away –

And now the farmer heard the bellowing bullocks. "God! you blind fool!" shot from his mouth (the farmer meant himself but the girl did not know this). "You bloody cows!" the farmer yelled and he left the cowshed in one bound. Emotion, who'd been hovering above the blonde, fell like a stone into her open mouth and lodged like a gob in her throat, threatening to choke her. Immediately she gave a strangled cry, but the farmer never heard, nor did he once look back. No, with Trouble there he was already running to the house with one thought in his mind: he must fetch his dear wife to help.

Indoors the diplomat was whispering sleekily into the ear of the farmer's wife, soft words conveying to her many things. The farmer's wife grew beautiful, as though she were a work of art rather than a farmer's mate. His lips engaged her ear, and now he whispered that his bullet wound necessitated that he rest his leg and when did she expect the farmer back from market?

But as he spoke the words quite suddenly they all blew back into his face and scattered in the air like specks of dust dancing on a sunbeam. Looking at the farmer's wife, he saw Distraction scattering her wits and Shock pull up her brows like catapults. Turning towards the object of her gaze he saw the farmer at the window peering in. How much could the farmer see? He did not wait in order to be told, but tore himself neatly from the farmer's wife, much as a shredder tears secret information when an embassy's in flight. As he did so four words flew from the farmer's mouth: "Bullocks in the silage!"

Never had the diplomat handled a farmer's wife before. Instead of the soft, rounded female form the four words 'Bullocks in the silage!' produced a tightly sprung coil; instead of the quiet, caressing voice that charmed came a klaxon pitched two octaves higher. This schizophrenic creature, no longer the princess, spat a great oath from her mouth like a peach-stone, sprang like a frog from his grasp and was gone.

Two seconds later he saw five bullocks in the yard. He saw the farmer's wife dash past the window, half in and half out of her gum-boots but pulling at them as she ran; and then he saw her stop. Why? Why did she stop dead and stare at something up the yard? Disbelief pulled down her jaw and made her gape. But soon the bullocks in a bunch moved off and she gave chase again. He saw the farmer leaping forward with a stick to block one exit, then springing to another to block that, before hurling the stick towards his wife who caught it on the run as together they vanished after their livelihood.

A moment passed, and then the blonde of great allure came into view. She stumbled down the yard buttoning her clothes and fled past the farmhouse choking from Emotion, her face averted, hoping to go unobserved but clearly seen. Soon she was gone as well.

Disappointment, like a wet flannel, covered the face of the despairing diplomat. He sat, or rather slumped, down on a chair. At times he held his head in his hands, at times he ran his fingers through his hair, and at other times he moved a hand over his noble features. Sin and Passion now were far away. Had he only been a pawn, used by Passion in some game, he wondered? Could Sin so quickly occupy his mind, only to depart as swiftly, when a bunch of bullocks got into the silage? A diplomat and farmer's wife, was it so foolish? At last he heaved a heavy sigh and rose and found his stick and left.

Later that evening, in the warm comfort of his home, Prude offered him his wife's thin cheek to kiss; its meagre familiarity comforted him a little. But a slight whiff of dung made the woman's nostrils flare. At once Prude sat his wife down and proceeded to open and shut her mouth as if it were a cat-flap through which questions leapt. Taking courage from a glass of Scotch the diplomat replied with suitably slick sentences designed to satisfy her curiosity. Prude, of course, did not believe a word of it and, taking his wife to bed early, soon had her fast asleep and snoring her contempt.

Back on the farm the Battle of the Cowshed was imminent. The bullocks had been rounded up, the big-bagged silage all re-bagged. The time was after ten o'clock at night. And, as the farmer fed hay to the small calves and his wife shovelled nuts to them, armies of words: verbs, nouns adjectives and adverbs, were circling round and round the confined space of their two heads. Suspicion had the farmer's troops under his command, whilst Indignation led the wilder bunch of accusations fighting for the farmer's wife.

The first salvo came from the angry woman – straight off the top of her head in a most undisciplined manner. Indignation tried to hold her tongue but without success. "Not to tie the hurdles! what were you bloody thinking of?" And Indignation made the woman glare at the stronghold of the farmer's face.

Suspicion gave nothing away; these skirmishes fully

satisfied him that his own forces were superior. Columns of words were lining up behind the battlements of the farmer's head, ready to emerge at a moment's notice. He decided now to take the opposition by surprise; this he knew from past experience always brought the best results. Selecting a bunch of good fighting words, he sent them out under Major Allegation to draw the enemy fire:

"I've had a letter from the bank."

So unexpected was this that General Indignation (whose noise and bluster usually served him well) was caught off-guard. In his confusion he could think of nothing better than to fire a pronoun in the air:

"What?"

"Our joint account's been blocked."

"What?" All routes from the woman's head seemed barred.

"They've bounced the cheque you wrote last week to buy your dress."

"What?"

To save the perilous situation Major Blame (one of Indignation's best fighters) seized the initiative and, grabbing a sharp remark out of the air, aimed it with great accuracy at the farmer:

"Money, money, money! It's all you ever think about!"

A rapid exchange of fire took place.

"Money's something you should think more about."

"I've better things to think about!"

"That's quite clear – I saw you through the window!"

This last volley produced a loud explosion. When the spluttering died down Major Reproach (another of Indignation's keen officers) rallied a small sentence with a trumpet charge and they all fell forward over the teeth of the farmer's wife with the cry:

"You always think the worst!"

"It doesn't help the farm when you go on like that."

"What should I do to help the farm, seduce the bloody bank manager?"

Allegation ricocheted an answer:

"You could do worse!"

A great flash came from the farmer's wife. Metal upon metal rang out as shovel and bucket struck the calf partitions and cattle-rearing nuts went flying through the air. A loose, erratic bunch of words shot from her tongue:

"You think I don't know why those bullocks all got out? You think I'm dumb like that blonde bitch of yours? Oh, yes! YOU had something on YOUR mind all right!"

Immediately the two armies locked themselves in bitter conflict. The farmer's wife opened up her mouth and a fusillade of words, horrible adjectives, lethal nouns, poured from her: an undisciplined mob of of military verbiage. General Suspicion responded with a thousand gibes and lambasted the woman with small, explosive charges of being 'unfaithful', 'disloyal', 'shameless', 'untrustworthy', 'frivolous', 'foolhardy' and 'useless'.

General Indignation, although losing ground, rallied his troops and fought back bravely. He responded with a cannonade of dialogue and a hundred arrows of accusation, some of which landed wide of the mark such as 'farmyard habits', 'smell of dung' and 'lonely insect-like existence', while others found their target such as 'boring grumbling farmers', and 'my mother warned me'.

With 'my mother warned me' Suspicion swung the farmer's head around as though it were a musket firing at a pheasant:

"Your mother! Too bad she didn't warn ME! A wife learning Greek is a real help to a farmer!"

Blame hurled back a sharp reply:

"And it's a real help to his wife when a farmer lets his bloody bullocks out!"

The battle now was at its height; the noise was audible across the valley. Both sides were firing simultaneously; each had the other in his sites and triggered fearful poisoned darts and wounding words:

"He made me feel quite feminine again. I liked it."

"Loved it, you mean."

"Yes, loved it! When he saw me carrying a bucket he took if from me!"

"Of course he bloody took it, he'd nothing else to do but flirt with you."

"He made me feel of consequence."

"Oh, he knew how to sweep you off your feet all right! And he couldn't wait to take the weight off his – your limping lover! He only had to take a bucket from you and he had you eating out of his soft hand like any bloody calf!"

"Don't you lecture me about soft hands when you've been groping after you-know-whose!"

Suddenly from the barrel of the farmer's mouth came a Guffaw. The Guffaw spun through the air and swirled and coiled around the woman opposite like a lassoo:

"You're your mother's daughter all right – always the last word! God, you're funny!"

Blame and Reproach reeled back under this unexpected whiplash, but Indignation held his ground and gave a sharp-tongued answer:

"Oh, ha! you always had a rotten sense of humour!"

Now Silence descended, falling quite suddenly between them like a dead bird between two dogs. And Indignation tied the woman's tongue and sealed her lips trying to keep Silence; and on the other side Suspicion observed Silence and waited, knowing Indignation would quite soon explode. And so he did:

"I suppose you said to your bum blonde: 'Don't bother – DARLING – I can't afford to pay you, so I'll get my sodding wife to help!'" And a flare shot up from the farmer's wife lighting up the dark night sky.

Seeing all things clearly suddenly, Suspicion tried a line of reasonable vocabulary and sent it marching out to call a truce under Major Condescension.

"Let's forget it, shall we? It's been a tiring day. We forgot the hurdles but all's well that – "

But one word had carelessly exposed itself and Indignation pounced on it at once:

"We? WE?" And Indignation stamped himself about the woman's face and cast a red glow burning on her cheeks.

"WE? WE?"

And Blame and Reproach capitalised and emphasised and underlined and sprayed the air with exclamation marks and many lines of dots and dashes:

"Not WE! OHHHHH, no! NOT WE!!!!!!!! YOU!!!!!!! I've spent ELEVEN HOURS rebagging sodding silage bags because of YOU!!!!!!!!!!!! GOD!!!!! what a WASTE OF TIME!!!!! And not ONE WORD of thanks for it! NOOOOOOO THANKS at all!!!!!! ELEVEN HOURS OF SLOG and have I heard a word of thanks???? NOT ONE!!!! NOOOO thanks!!!!!

Suspicion fired a round of biting Sarcasm into her ear as she paused an instant to draw breath:

"A dead language but a live lover – and I'm to thank you? Had I caught you with a book you would have shouted 'what?' or 'wait!' or 'go away!' Instead you came out like a scalded cat – and I'm to thank YOU?"

But Indignation blocked her ears and this biting

Sarcasm went straight over her head.

Blame and Reproach redoubled their efforts at the jaws of the woman:

"…All right BLAME ME!!!!!! I'm the one at fault! I'm the one who goes too far in EVERYTHING… who's written the ONE cheque that BOUNCED… Go on! You're just the POOR HARD-DONE-BY farmer verging on the brink of bankcruptcy because of MEEEEE!!!!! Nothing YOU do is EVER wrong, oh, NOOOOO…YOU'RE just the farmer who LOVES any show of wild ENTHUSIASM – who just goes CRAZY over nutty blondes because THEY give FREELY of their time! Though when they're REALLY NEEEEEEEDED because the bullocks have got out AND ALL the silage bags are ripped, they get the hell out of it, DON'T THEY!!!! I saw her BLUBBING DOWN THE YARD…POOR THING!!!!!! I WONDER WHY? Because you'd made her HAPPY??????? Or had you said to her: 'Oh, sorry – DARLING!!!! – now I've WORK to do so now I NEED MY WIFE!!!!!!'"

General Suspicion kept within the shelter of the farmer's head while this bombardment was kept up. He knew that Indignation's fighting forces always started off with energy but would exhaust themselves – and this proved to be the case. As the flak died down, Suspicion seized his opportunity. He gave the order and immediately a sharp two-edged remark was flung and found its target:

"You have to work at marriage if you want it to succeed!"

Indignation pulled the woman's face into a fearful scowl:

"Work? My God! Haven't I been working?"

A second remark aimed at her heart flew from

Suspicion's lines:

"Believe it or not I love you!"

"Indignation fired a wild retort:

"Love me? Then you've a bloody awful way of showing it!"

Two finely pointed sentences flew through the air and now sank home:

"If loving you and working hard on your behalf is a bloody awful way of showing it, then bloody awful it will have to be! But still I LOVE YOU!"

General Indignation felt the puff go out of him and his letters visibly shrank. Blame and Reproach tried to rally some support but their best nouns and verbs were already in full flight. A stream of words charged straight into their broken lines striking at what followers remained: first Beast and Rotter fell to Tenderness, then Brute and Cad collapsed as Kindness mowed them down, and Fib was chased and killed by Truth, while extravagance who saw Prudence coming for him, turned and ran back into the head of the farmer's wife.

General Indignation, deflated beyond all recognition, prayed that his reserves would arrive in time; but his array of nouns and verbs and all his best fighters were utterly disseminated. Blame and Reproach tried to work the woman's tongue around two words 'damn you!' but she was altogether inarticulate and they died together on her lips. Only a few useless stragglers remained such as 'and', 'but', 'so', 'if'. These staggered bravely amongst floundering letters and scattered punctuation marks before falling in their tracks.

General Suspicion was triumphant. His front line had held and he went forward to victory, the well-trained nouns and verbs marching neatly out in a long, unbeatable sentence:

"I love you! Like it or not you are my wife. And as a farmer's wife you ought to know by now the animals must come first!"

There was no answering volley, no sharp retort as words failed the farmer's wife. Instead a white handkerchief was taken out and she covered her face with it as a symbol of complete surrender.

Later that night – much later – penetrating the blackness of the night a 'cri de coeur' was heard. Not long after it was heard again. Love, Comfort, Honour and Keep, who were huddled together and almost fossilised inside a prayer book, stirred stiffly and came to. Again the 'cri de coeur' was heard and this time they looked at one another and without more ado they left the pages of the prayer book.

The nocturnal darkness bore them up as together they headed for this 'cri de coeur'. They came to rest above the farmhouse where the farmer and his wife were tossing restlessly back and forth beneath the bed-clothes of their double bed. Love, Comfort, Honour and Keep, like a secret squad on a rescue mission, stole down the chimney and sprang silently into action. They bound the farmer and his wife hand and foot together and plunged a knife into the 'cri de coeur' and silenced it. Love, Comfort, Honour and Keep felt life breathe back into the couple. There they all were in the pitch black of the night, and there they all were as the sun rose on the farm next day.

Thus it was that over the next months the farmer and his wife stayed on the farm together and trod the fields together hand in hand. And they dealt bills to each other as though they were a pack of cards; and read their bank statements, and studied their overdrafts and felt the insignificance of such things whilst Love, Comfort, Honour and Keep kept vigil over them for a while.

It was, of course, only a matter of time before once again the farmer's wife was seen sitting on a bale of straw reading a book – yes, Scholarship was back and Diversion was not very far away. And, beating the bounds from east to west, from south to north, diagonally across his fields and so on, could be discerned the farmer's legs twinkling beneath the shadow of a large sombrero hat as it moved rapidly around the fields like a flying-saucer – yes, Determination was back as well.

But by now the Battle of the Cowshed was written – words had seen to it. Such words! Such valiant words! all demanding that no effort should be spared to tell the world about the bitter struggle that had taken place. They laid themselves on paper, competing with each other for the honour of a place; each one wanting to contribute to posterity; to do honour to the memory of the one and only glorious battle of its kind: The Battle of the Cowshed.

A HOLIDAY IN VENICE

A holiday! From the moment that the flight was booked Time rolled forward like a swirling cloud to the week, the day, the hour, the very moment of departure.

A holiday! The farmer fenced and fussed and found a youth prepared to feed his cattle for the days he would be gone – three days.

A holiday! At last Time swirled and swept the farmer from the farm. Time, like a stork carrying a cradle through the sky, flew over the wide world bearing the farmer and his wife together with their 'expectations' – all travellers have 'expectations': the farmer's wife of happiness, the farmer of expenditure.

Mammon, the small god of riches whom the farmer worshipped, had persuaded him a few months back to raise his overdraft to buy young stock. He would make a profit, so he was told, and so they would but one had died. But with the hope the rest would live the farmer took this holiday urged on by his loving wife. Often Mammon fuddled human minds this way, weaving into them financial wizardry which then would go awry.

A holiday! They landed in a fog – not a thick London fog but a soft Venetian autumn one. They crossed the tarmac clutching packages, each traveller himself a carefully packaged character. Hunting together in a pack like hounds sniffing the warm air, sometimes going in circles, sometimes doubling back, they finally found the trail and headed for the water-bus.

And now Time took them to the heart of Venice; the farmer's wife alert and looking everywhere, the farmer counting the cost of the journey. They were taken round the wide lagoon, past the small islands of Murano, Burano and Torcello; then around the headland passing the Lido until there! not on a canvas nor in a brochure nor in a dream, but there in reality, lay before them the domed outline of the Salute della San Maria, the campanile and church on the island of San Giorgio; there the palazzos, ancient, dilapidated, yet supremely proud in their Gothic tracery with their crenellated roof-tops, their crumbling walls lapped by the waters of the Grand Canal where vaporetti, barges and the many water-taxis were busy furrowing their way; and there a gondola and gondolier in silhouetted outline, seemingly fastened to the water like a badge of office proudly borne on some breast.

A holiday! At last Time took them to their destination, to their hotel. The stocky, olive-faced receptionist, well groomed, black hair brushed back, expressionless, regarded over his bifocals the pink faced English farmer. He eyed the laced-up boots and fishing hat. Ah, yes, from England – a message. The outer wrappings of the farmer's character flew off. He read the note. His mother, left in charge of small domestic pets, was worried – no relief worker had come to feed the cattle. The farmer clapped a hand to his head.

The farmer's wife said: "Oh, God! I suppose that means you're going back?" And Mammon, like a dervish, began a stately dance, winding himself in and out of all their minds in slow and measured convolutions. The farmer, in high tension wondered how he could return. He thought of supplementary payments, cancellations and the cost of international phone calls. He thought of his soaring overdraft which, like a hawk gone skywards he hoped to keep hovering where it was until he sold some barren cows.

Over his bifocals the receptionist eyed first one, then the other. Soft hands from black jacket sleeves shuffled a few papers as he waited for decisions to be made. The farmer's wife said suddenly: "Well, I'm not going back, not now we've got here. Now we're here I'm seeing Venice!" and he saw her flying jacket sweep out through the revolving doors of the hotel.

Enraged that the farm, like an octopus, had shot out a tentacle and snatched the farmer back a prisoner, the farmer's wife set off alone to see the sights. Mammon accompanied her to the edge of the Piazza where she saw for the first time the hunched, domed splendour of St. Mark's Basilica with its glistening, gilded portals. At once anxiety, fury and frustration fell from her and, as though sprouting wings, she approached the divine edifice.

Inside was half-light and shadow. Soft, glowing, wine-red lamps hung suspended and above them glistened domes of magnificent mosaics depicting brilliant coloured scenes of biblical significance. She trod the fine mosaics on the ground, walking where the feet of doges, foreign monarchs, popes and poets had all passed before. She stood before two peacocks in mosaics, divinely brought to life in coloured marble, with a tracery of arabesques surrounding them, the whole contained within fine geometric patterns spreading outwards from them. She sat at peace and revelled at the splendour, the holy aura holding her uplifted and quite motionless.

And all the while Mammon revolved spectral fashion, commanding worship of such riches, commanding honour and respect until inwardly the farmer's wife cried out: "What inspiration! what creation! Without wealth how could this have come about?" And, as Mammon passed an arm around her and revolved away again, she cried inwardly a second time: "First wealth! wealth rewarding genius with its creative powers – those two! those two alone bring such vision from the mind into reality!" Mammon whirled past once more and the woman, bright-eyed, looked around and then cried inwardly a third time: "And labour! without labour what can wealth and genius do? How necessary is the hierarchy of things!"

She paid to see the gem-encrusted, gold-wrought altar screen: and paid again to see the four bronze Grecian horses – the fine, victorious booty from some past crusade; these majestic beasts stood at the prance, flared nostrils neighing their energy and impatience to be gone. The farmer's wife looked around ready to share with anyone her own enthusiasms. A middle-aged Italian, grey-haired and noble featured, soon offered her the benefit of his superior knowledge.

And, because she wished to hear and he had much to say, they wandered out together into the Piazza where a small orchestra was playing. They sat in basket chairs and he asked to be allowed to buy her coffee. Waiters in white jackets weaved between the tables bearing trays above their shoulders. And, as they sat and talked St. Mark's Basilica, in hunched splendour, watched discreetly from under gilded lids.

"A farmer's wife?" the middle-aged Italian asked, "so you make your own butter and your own cheese?" "No," she answered, "I learn Greek, play the guitar and read." "You do?" he asked, "Oh, but you must tell me all about yourself!" and at once told her all about himself instead. He said he was a widower and he had come on holiday to exorcise his sorrow; that he lived in Milan and had a grown family.

The farmer's wife was not a woman of the world. From deep within her packaged self were hidden longings to be daring and adventurous. A middle-aged and knowledgeable Italian guiding her round Venice? Oh, yes! In three days' time she would be back in England on the farm. Would she return regretting missed opportunities? No, she would not! The confiding voice told her how he'd walk her around Venice that same evening if she found her husband having to fly home again – a little walk, nothing too strenuous, she would be tired, of course, after her long journey, nevertheless, if she would like to, it would be his pleasure.

Back at the hotel she found the farmer, like a waxwork, reclining on his bed with the telephone receiver to his ear. "It's wonderful! quite wond – " she began, but he silenced her with a gesture. The farmer's wife bristled.

And, because he was concerned with telephoning to make adequate arrangements on the farm; and because, between speaking on the phone he pointed to a paper bag containing rolls and ham and said that that could be their supper, she took herself off to join the middle-aged Italian who was sitting down below puffing smoke-rings thoughtfully from a large cigar.

It was now dark. She must, he told her, see the Rialto

Bridge by night. And if she would allow him to introduce her to Venetian food, he knew a trattoria where they could eat. And so they took a vaporetti to the Rialto Bridge. The Grand Canal was alive with boats churning up the lapping waters, disturbing the reflected lights, roughing up the black silhouetted movements of the gondolas whose gondoliers with their forward sweeping action steered on their high-prowed vessels from the rear. The golden light of the floodlit Rialto Bridge came into view while the ancient palazzos stood crumblingly resplendent either side, self-lovingly reflected in the waters.

He was so very charming, her companion. They sat at a trattoria and his well-bred opulence pleased her, while her appreciation of such things enchanted him. "Oh, by the way," the middle-aged Italian said, and put a smooth hand into his breast pocket and withdrew a well-tooled leather wallet. Did she like opera, he asked? Yes, he could see she did. He had a ticket for the La Fenice Theatre the next night. He had business he must attend all day, but if she would in the evening keep him company and see the most beautiful theatre in all Europe, he would be honoured. No, no, he would not dream of taking money for it – it was his pleasure.

And so the middle-aged Italian, immaculately dressed, walked with her back to her hotel. They wandered down alleyways, over narrow bridges looping gracefully across dark, glinting waterways made sombre by the occasional black gondola sliding silently along with its single light fastened like a glow-worm to the prow. The shuttered windows of the high-walled houses seemed mysteriously unwakeful, untroubled by the tourists after dark or the quick purposeful step of the Venetian going home. An occasional muzzled dog straining at its leash came by drawing its owner after it.

When she got back to her hotel she found the farmer more relaxed. What was Venice like, he asked? As she began to speak he told her of his fears concerning hazards on the farm which might kill or maim the relief worker he had arranged to come. He told her of his tractor with a faulty brake which made it veer off to the left; and another which would only start if run downhill; and a ladder in the hay barn with a lethal rung. And, as the farmer's wife got into bed he told her of two mangy calves he was ashamed of because they should have been de-loused, and a bullock he was more ashamed of still with a wart hanging from its stomach as large as any pineapple. At this his wife screamed 'stop!' and put a pillow on her head. Wondering what was the matter with her, the farmer got into his bed too and cast himself beneath the bedclothes. Stretching out an arm he switched the light off, hoping that next day his wife would be in better humour.

But because at breakfast the farmer told her all his troubles once again and said that he must telephone the farm and check on his insurance, his wife exploded, flung down her table-napkin and took herself off alone to explore the Left Bank of the Grand Canal.

She took a vaporetti to the Church of San Maria della Salute but found it huge and bare compared with the Basilica. She tried to find the Palazzo Rezzonico but lost her way. She wandered down alleyways where there were greengrocers and butchers and busy housewives shopping. She came across glass-blowers working their sensitive powers on small rods of coloured glass. She passed small shops with strange masks mocking her and others full of carved and gilded frames, and others still with lace and fine embroidery. She looked up at the bulbous wrought-iron balconies and window-shutters thrown open to the autumn sun and to lines of washing. She crossed cobbled squares and went down dead-ends to find herself beside the Grand Canal again with no means of walking alongside and so she was obliged to turn back on her tracks.

It began to rain. And so she took a vaporetti and went back across the Grand Canal to the hotel to fetch an anorak. The receptionist handed her the key. Eyeing her above his bifocals he said ambiguously: "A most devoted farmer!" A note in the bedroom said: "Gone exploring." She was surprised. She also left a note saying: "Gone exploring too!"

She sat down at a trattoria under a large green umbrella around the fringe of which the rain dripped relentlessly – a warm Venetian rain, not a cold English one. She ate spaghetti Bolognese and had a glass of wine to cheer herself. Was it not her fault she sat alone? For a while she sat there studying her guide-book.

And now the sun came out again and so she went up the Campanile to see the panoramic views. She gazed across the russet coloured roof tops and over the green leaded domes of St. Mark's Basilica. An old blind pigeon strutted round the ledge beside her; some corn had been left out for him and he pecked blindly with his beak until he found a grain. The farmer's wife commiserated with him and pushed another grain before him before staring out once more across the roofs and vista stretching out before her.

She looked down at the Piazza and watched the people ambling and gazing all about them. It was at that moment that she saw him! There he was in his fishing hat and laced-up boots. He was springing along and at his side was a girl with a madonna face, wearing a long cotton skirt

– she could have been a ballet dancer the way she moved. They were talking animatedly together, waving their hands expressively. Neither looked at the Basilica or the shop windows along the arcade. They disappeared in the direction of the Grand Canal. Dark thoughts descended on the farmer's wife until she remembered that she too was there on holiday and that night was going to the opera.

She set off for the Doge's Palace. Too much, too much! each room more sumptuous than the last. She traversed a hall of gigantic length and width, every square inch of wall and ceiling depicting fearful scenes of battle: of horses rearing, tumbling, neighing, galloping; of men dying, killing, staggering, collapsing, screaming, wounding; while high above stared the serene faces of past Doges. She sat down on a bench along one wall while Mammon made use of the long hall, whirling and swirling its full length. She tried to take in what was visible before her but the extent and breadth of that great hall; the longitude and latitude; the depths and heights; the wealth of oils and colours; the profusion of soft brush-strokes sweeping and circling and creating and fixing! No, no! It was genius let loose under the patronage of Doges! the mass production of what wealth could buy! Yes! Mammon twirled and whirled bewildering the common mind and bringing from the farmer's wife a heavy sigh – deep-felt, heart-felt, almost a groan.

When she emerged into the Piazza once again she saw the evening would be fine. After studying her guide book she set off to find the Palazzo Contarini staircase. After finding herself down dead-ends, in ancient courtyards, down back alleyways; having crossed numerous canals and countless bridges; after having been directed in opposite directions by those with muzzled dogs and shopping bags, she gave up the search and went back to the hotel.

There she found another note: "Being taken round fruit and veg. market at the Rialto. Expect me when you see me." She left a note saying: "Being taken to La Fenice Theatre. Ditto." And as she prepared herself, Mammon danced smoothly and, with extended hands, drew on her face a subtle bloom, and gave her modest clothes an air of opulence. Then, with an arm about her he guided her attentively to the rich beauty of the La Fenice Theatre where the middle-aged Italian was already waiting for her.

They entered this small jewel-box of a theatre and sat in elegant tub-chairs upholstered in rose velvet. Curved around the auditorium were tiers of small gilded opera boxes, lit by a thousand wall-sconces, each box adorned by frescoes of nymphs and shepherds in pastel shades amidst carved and gilded garlands. Facing the stage was the state box, larger and more ornate and graced by more works of art on walls and ceiling and framed in red velvet fastened back by golden tasselled cords. And on the garlanded and frescoed ceiling there hung a chandelier whose hundred brilliant lights fanned outwards like a hundred brilliant dewdrops drawing attention to the bucolic scenes above. Embedded on the ceiling near the stage was a round clock as elegant as the finest wrist-watch. And on the painted Safety Curtain was portrayed a Doge stepping from his state gondola, being welcomed by dignitaries outside the Doge's Palace.

The opera itself was exquisitely incomprehensible. Arias and action fusing time past with the eternal present. As they emerged afterwards, the middle-aged Italian took the elbow of the farmer's wife, telling her he knew the very place to go after the opera. If she would do him the honour of keeping him company over dinner then he would see her back to her hotel. And as he spoke he used his hands expressively, his eyes confiding to his lips a little moue of possiblities.

From their table under a striped awning they could see an arched bridge and a dark alleyway beyond. Small lighted windows displayed Venetian glass, strange masks and leather goods. From a distant canal there floated the faint strains of a romantic melody: a tenor voice, accompanied by an accordianist, was singing a serenade. Every now and then a second voice joined in with short drunken snatches, followed by a girl's laughter. The sound grew nearer until the black silhouetted outline of a gondola slid into view, its glow-worm light to the fore. The hunched figure of the accordianist sat in the bows and beside him stood an olive-faced Venetian in a straw boater with a ribbon, hand on heart and singing 'O Sole Mio'. The gondolier, with his wide sweeping forward thrust, brought on the gondola towards them.

The farmer's wife first saw the fishing hat. She saw the farmer with his face hidden in the long hair of the girl with the madonna face. In an instant she had sprung up and shouted: "Hey, you!" which caused the diners to look round as did the farmer. He reacted as though he had been punched and scrambled to his feet. Seeing his wife he called back unsteadily: "Oh, hello, darling, so that's where you've got to!" and immediately he lost his balance. With a fine display of bending one way, then another, then buckling at the knees and grabbing anything to hand he seized hold of the coat of his companion and fell overboard taking her with him. The tenor lost his balance too and with a mighty splash was overboard as well, whilst the accordianist sat tight, bowing his body protectively over his accordian.

What turmoil! What confusion! All Venice seemed to gather shouting volubly. The tenor re-emerged, spitting water, and swam in a circle spluttering with rage. Then, with strong, angry strokes he made for the bridge. Extended arms reached for the struggling, gasping girl who, when not gulping water, screamed and laughed alternately. The middle-aged Italian hurried forward authoritatively, one arm out whilst trying to keep his dapper trousers dry. Another, stronger arm drew the girl from the water on to the walkway where she fell into the arms of the middle-aged Italian who embraced, petted, soothed and took her sodden body leaning limply on his breast to a chair put forward for her. He seemed to have forgotten all about the farmer's wife who anyway had quite forgotten him as she watched the farmer seize his sodden fishing hat and swim away into the darkness.

Darting over bridges and following the line of the canal she shouted after him: "Oh, stop! Come back!" After some hundred metres in the canal, and several hundred metres of twisting alleyways and bridges, in a dark corner of the canal, she saw the farmer reach up for the walk-way and heave his soaking body out. Hurrying to him she put a protective arm around him and, like two conspirators, they ran away together into the darkness.

The receptionist was again on duty that night. Over his bifocals he saw the wet figure of the farmer leaving sloppy foot prints in the hallway. Immediately he took command. Unsmiling, he came from behind his desk, his eyes on this wet bedragglement making a mockery of his hotel. Flicking his fingers to right and left minions came running. The farmer and his wife were bundled out of sight and sent up in the lift whilst all traces of their foot prints were quickly mopped away.

The hotel dealt with the farmer's clothes and his wife dealt with his person. After a hot bath he sat in his pyjamas, a vulnerable figure with his hair on end. The farmer's wife sat opposite then, as though rubbing him down with a rough towel, she cried: "A gondola! when I said let's take a gondola you said you'd rather buy a wheelbarrow with a pneumatic tyre or a new aluminium ladder! A gondola! and with a tenor and an accordianist! that must have cost a load of hay!" "I was thinking of you," the farmer said. "And what about that woman?" The farmer, shrinking into his pyjamas, said: "She told me she was interested in the marketing of milk in England." "Oh, was she just!" his wife retorted. "I thought we'd come to get away from farming for three days – to have a holiday together!" "I thought so too, but you were never there." "That's wonderful!" his wife replied, "you think of me but go off with another woman. I really like to know you're thinking about me when another woman takes my place!" And the farmer's wife suddenly felt miserable and flung herself on to the bed and curled up in a ball.

From the walkway outside their window they heard voices and loud laughter as a group of men passed by discussing something; their footsteps receded with their laughter. At last the farmer's wife turned her face towards the farmer: "Why don't you ask what I was doing? Much you care about that!" she said. "I do care, that's why I don't ask," the farmer answered. "So that's how you show you care? You care but don't ask and go out in a gondola taking another woman with you? It's just what a girl likes to be told. She likes to hear her husband cares about her but goes out with another woman in a gondola!" And she curled up in a ball again as once more footsteps outside passed by accompanied by a woman's voice rising in pitch until it burst into a peal of laughter and was joined by a male companion.

Ten minutes later the farmer again spoke. "I only did it because I didn't think you cared. Three days here worrying about the farm – " "Don't mention that word!" And the farmer's wife sprang off the bed. But now she took the farmer's hands. She drew him to his feet and the strings that had been tying them in knots undid themselves; the wrappings which for long had hidden many thoughts and feelings fell away. What for long had lain dormant beneath thick layers of covering was miraculously discovered once again.

And if Mammon had been dancing in attendance putting reminders into their heads of the pleasures of extravagance and the worries of too much extravagance; of caring over much about frivolity or of caring not enough; he now found himself superfluous and slunk away defeated and forgotten – for the time being anyway.

Next morning the receptionist, leaning over an open newspaper before him, followed over his bifocals the progress of the farmer and his wife from the lift doors to the dining-room. When they had disappeared he sighed inwardly (never outwardly) then went on reading the headlines. But, as he read, into his mind there flitted the vision of the farmer swimming the canal and, despite himself, rather like a regurgitating bovine beast, there came across his face a muzzled smile.

That day the farmer and his wife explored Venice together. They meandered through a maze of alleyways; found hidden squares and ancient churches. They crossed arched narrow bridges over waterways; leaned over carved parapets and watched the gloomy waters lapping at the stones of buildings either side. They watched a Venetian step from his front-door into his motor-boat, untie it from its moorings and chug away. They heard the siren of a swiftly moving red fire-boat speeding down the Grand Canal. They could feel the reflected glory of the past and the mysterious magic of the present day. They basked in the light and colour thrown like a soft mantle over Venice. They leaned against wrought-iron parapets and gazed up at leaded domes and russet coloured roof tops; and they turned and leaned over the same parapet and looked down into the dark waters of the canal. And, as they idled, loitered and meandered, Venice enticed, entwined and embraced them, making them hers.

And just as Time had whirled them up and brought them there on holiday, so Time drew them away again. It was evening when they caught their motor-launch to take them to the airport. They watched Venice's receding outline darkening: the silhouetted domes, the campanile and church on the island of San Giorgio; the Gothic tracery and crenellations of the palazzos all reflected in the waters of the Grand Canal. Beacon lamps on posts guided them away towards the Lido, bringing them rudely into the world of cars and motor-coaches again.

In the Piazza gas lamps flickered and came on along the length of the arcade. Two orchestras were playing, vying with each other. The middle-aged Italian, sitting in a basket chair, kept his eyes on the madonna-faced young girl seated opposite. He fondled her soft hand, using the gentle art of tenderness and the subtle lure of opulence to keep her volatile attention. Had he not allowed her latitude the day before so that he might rein her in a little tighter to him now? Had he not paid for her that evening on the gondola to indulge her whim?

He threaded his fingers through the girl's as she prattled her adventures to him. "He was a farmer," she was telling him. The middle-aged Italian seemed surprised.

"That's strange," he said reflectively. "She was a farmer's wife!"

And as the truth dawned on them and as the orchestras played on and people wandered and admired, slowly, imperceptibly, in discreet flood-lighting, St. Mark's Basilica lit up a violet pink, its arched portals glistening gold.